FLOWERS
FOR EVERYONE

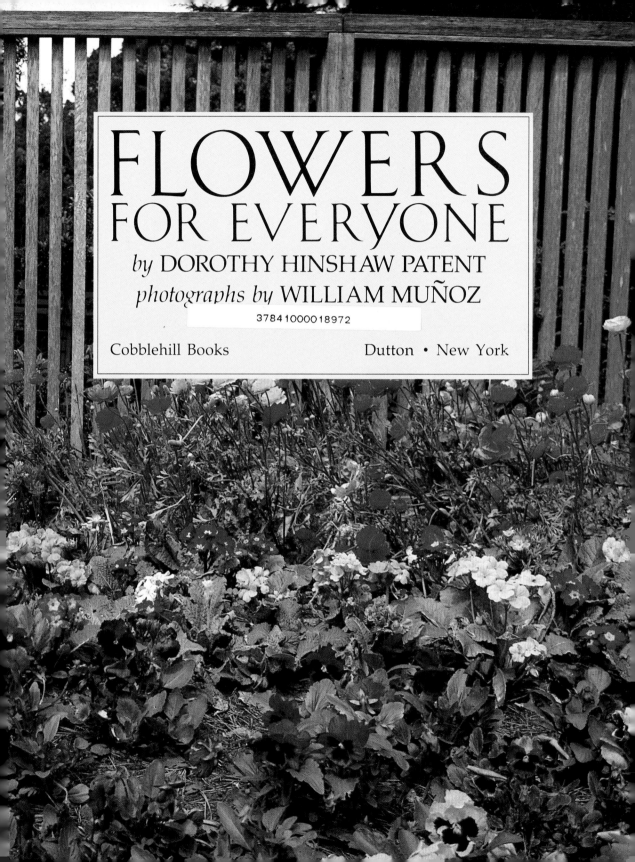

FLOWERS
FOR EVERYONE

by DOROTHY HINSHAW PATENT

photographs by WILLIAM MUÑOZ

Cobblehill Books   Dutton • New York

For our sister and friend,
Barbara Baird,
who loves flowers.

Acknowledgments

The author and photographer wish to thank the following people and companies for their help with this book—Adrienne Mellon, John Muller, Peter Barr, Eric Jaeger, Donna King Davenport, Nancy and David Cavanaugh, Goldsmith Seeds, Cavanaugh Color, Acres of Orchids, Jeff Brothers, and Exotics Hawaii-Kona Inc.

Text copyright © 1990 by Dorothy Hinshaw Patent
Photographs copyright © 1990 by William Muñoz

Library of Congress Cataloging-in-Publication Data
Patent, Dorothy Hinshaw.
  Flowers for everyone / Dorothy Hinshaw Patent ; photographs by William Muñoz.
    p.   cm.
  Summary: Discusses the significance, growth, and cultivation of flowers and examines
    specific kinds.
  ISBN 0-525-65025-3
  1. Flowers—Juvenile literature.   2. Plants, Ornamental—Juvenile literature.
    3. Floriculture—Juvenile literature. [1. Flowers.] I. Muñoz, William, ill. II. Title.
SB406.5.P37   1990
635.9—dc20   89-23937
                                                                                          CIP
                                                                                           AC

Published in the United States by
Cobblehill Books, an affiliate of Dutton Children's Books,
a division of Penguin Books USA Inc.
Published simultaneously in Canada by
Fitzhenry & Whiteside Limited, Toronto
Designer: Jean Krulis
Printed in Hong Kong   First Edition
10   9   8   7   6   5   4   3   2   1

CONTENTS

ONE
Beauty and Meaning

Everyone loves flowers. A bunch of dandelions or wild flowers is often the first present children proudly give to their mothers. Flowers have been gifts of friendship and sympathy for hundreds of years, and giving them on special occasions is a custom in many countries.

Flowers have meant different things to people through the ages. The name of the familiar blue forget-me-not comes from its symbolic meaning as a loving remembrance, while daisies stand for innocence.

Red, yellow, blue, or white, flowers of any color look lovely to us. Flowers are so much a part of our idea of beauty that it's difficult to imagine them not being appreciated in this way. But in Europe, gardens were not planted for pleasure until the sixteenth century. Plants—even those with pretty flowers—were grown only for the food they produced or to provide medicines or dyes.

Overleaf: Daisies are a symbol of innocence.

Flowers as Medicine

Before modern medicine, people used familiar plants, many of them flowers, to treat injuries and diseases. Tea brewed from dried parsley flowers was used to treat skin ailments. Poppy flowers were added to cough remedies. Their bright red petals also served as a coloring in tea, wine, ink, and medicines. The common dandelion has been a very useful flower over time. Not only can its leaves and roots be eaten, its flowers make a fine yellow dye or wine. Even today, a quarter of our medicines are made from plants, many of them flowers. The petals from a pretty pink wild periwinkle that

Dandelions may be weeds to us, but their leaves and flowers actually have many uses.

grows on the island of Madagascar contain a strong cancer-fighter. The chemical is extracted from the flowers and used against Hodgkin's disease and childhood leukemia.

Flowers for Beauty

Late in the sixteenth century, Western Europe began to trade with the Ottoman Empire, centered in Turkey. European visitors to Turkey returned with stories about the spectacular gardens of the sultan, ruler of the Empire.

It wasn't long before big, beautiful cultivated flowers reached the West, and the idea of gardens as pleasing places to relax and to appreciate beauty became fashionable there. Ever since, people have enjoyed growing flowers just for their loveliness and their attractive scents.

Today, home flower gardening is more popular than growing vegetables. Vegetable crops usually require plenty of space. Almost anyone has room for a pot or window box full of lovely flowers, even in a small apartment.

Growing flowers and buying cut flowers to beautify the home are now so common that providing seeds, plants, and cut flowers is big business. How are the seeds grown? How do new flower varieties come into being? Where does the amazing variety of cut flowers come from?

The Origins of Garden Flowers

All our familiar garden flowers originally came from wild ones. Gardeners bred them for generations and generations, selecting the ones they liked best to grow the next year. Over

Roses have come a long way from their wild origins.

time, garden flowers became bigger and more colorful than their wild cousins. Wild roses, for example, are only an inch or two across and have only five modest petals. Their range of colors is also limited. Today's garden roses come in every shade of the rainbow, and their many-petaled blossoms can measure five to six inches.

The gladiolus comes in many sizes, colors, and flower types.

Left: Snapdragons are an old-fashioned flower now available in many different forms.

The original flowers from which cultivated snapdragons were developed grow wild in the Mediterranean area. The plants are perennials—plants that live for several years—that flower in the summer and can't stand very much cold. Garden snapdragons today are another matter. Not only is there an amazing variety of snapdragons for home gardens, there are also special varieties for greenhouse growing. Four different groups of these have been developed. One type blooms in the winter and early spring, while a second flowers during the summer. In late fall, another kind takes over. It can also be planted to bloom in the late spring. Finally, a fourth type blooms in late winter and spring. By growing these different kinds of snapdragons, a greenhouse grower can have snapdragons to sell to florists year around.

While many garden flowers were developed by improving on wild ones over generations, others came about through crossing wild species that normally wouldn't interbreed. The modern gladiolus resulted from the crossing of at least a dozen different related species with one another. Today, there are more than 10,000 garden varieties of this popular flower.

TWO
From Seed to Plant

New flower varieties are produced scientifically these days. If a seed company can come up with a better geranium or a more colorful petunia, it can make a lot of money. So a great deal of effort is spent deciding what new plants to come up with and to developing them. But to understand how this process is carried out, you first need to know some things about how plants make seeds.

What Is a Flower?

To us, a flower is a thing of beauty. For a plant, it's a way of making more plants. Most flowers have both male and female parts. The male parts are stamens, tiny stalks topped with knobs called anthers. The anthers are covered with fine yellow dust, the pollen grains. The pollen grains are like the sperm cells of animals.

The female part of the flower, called the pistil, is in the center. On top, the pistil has one or more stigmas, sticky

The geranium plant on the right is a new variety that produces many more flowers than older varieties, such as the one growing next to it.

surfaces where pollen grains attach. Deep inside the flower, at the base of the pistil, are the ovaries, with the egg cells to be fertilized. The proceess of getting the pollen from the male part of a flower to the female part is called pollination.

Most flowers are usually cross-pollinated—pollen from one flower is transferred to the stigma of a different blossom by a pollinator. Such flowers are constructed so that it is difficult for them to pollinate themselves. The stigma of some flowers becomes mature before the pollen is ripe. In others, the pistil sticks out of the flower above the stamens so that the pollen from the same flower can't easily reach it.

The pistils of these rhododendron flowers are long and curved. It's easy to see the enlarged stigmas on their tips and the short stamens with yellow-tipped anthers that surround the base of the stigma.

The bright colors of these ranunculus flowers help attract pollinators.

The bright colors of flowers and their lovely fragrances serve to attract bees and other pollinators such as hummingbirds. When a bee reaches into a flower to collect its nectar or pollen to take back to the hive, pollen sticks to its body. When it goes on to the next flower, some of the pollen brushes off onto the stigma of the flower, pollinating it. Each pollen grain then grows a long tube down through the style to the ovaries, where the egg cells are fertilized. The fertilized egg cells then develop into seeds.

The Remarkable Seed

Seeds are life suspended, which moisture and warmth will make grow. Many kinds of seeds will keep for years and sprout as soon as conditions are right. The seed has several

Flower seeds come in different sizes and shapes. Tiny snapdragon seeds are in the center. Starting at the top and going clockwise, the other seeds are nasturtiums, marigolds, zinnias, ornamental sunflowers, and pansies.

different parts. Inside, there is a tiny plant, called the embryo. If you carefully break a shelled peanut in half, you can see the tiny beginnings of the new plant between the two halves. Besides the embryo, the seed contains nourishment (the two halves of the peanut) that will allow the young plant to grow until it produces green leaves. Then the leaves can gather light energy to make their own food. A seed also has a tough outer coating to protect the embryo inside.

Making New Varieties

When a company that grows and sells flower seeds wants to come up with a new variety, the process takes six to twelve years. The first step is to decide on goals—for example, a small plant with many big flowers that blooms early. Then the plant breeder takes over. Seed companies have large collections of different seeds for the kinds of flowers they grow. One type may have big flowers while another one blooms very early. Still a third kind could have small plants. The trick it to combine all the desired traits into one variety.

Most people want to know just how their flower plants will turn out—how tall they'll be, when they will bloom, what color the flowers will be. They want all the plants of one kind to look the same. For these reasons, a plant breeder must work to make the plants that grow from the seeds as much alike as possible.

The best way to do this is to produce hybrid seed. Hybrids can only be bred with plants that have fairly large flowers, because the flowers must be pollinated by hand. And because the work involved is very expensive and time-consuming,

Yellow Sophia

Aurora
Yellow Fire

☆NEW☆

Left: Goldsmith Seeds, a commercial grower, runs trials in which new varieties are compared with old ones. Here, a new marigold is shown next to two older, similar varieties. The new one is more uniform from plant to plant.

These hundreds of pansy plants are virtually identical.

456 (3s)
x
3 25-(5)

only very popular flowers such as petunias and geraniums are usually hybridized.

To get hybrids, the breeder develops two different strains of the plant, a female strain and a male one. This can take months or even years. The female strain is inbred for generations until the plants look just the same. So is the male strain. The female strain plants look different from those of the male strain. Some of the desired traits are carried by each strain. Because they are so inbred, however, these parent plants are not very strong and don't grow very well. But when the pollen from the male strain is used to pollinate the flowers of the female, the resulting seeds grow into healthy plants that look alike—in this example, all are small plants with early blooming big flowers—and bloom at the same time.

Detail Work

Making sure that the flowers are pollinated properly while developing new varieties is tricky. Even though many flowers are designed so that self-pollination is difficult, some can still pollinate themselves if left alone. The plant breeder, however, wants only pollen from the male strain to pollinate the female strain when developing hybrid seed. For this reason, the anthers of each flower of the female strain must be removed before the pollen is ripe. With some kinds of flowers, it's possible to breed strains which don't produce pollen. The breeder can put this trait into the female parent strain. Then, there is no problem with self-pollination.

The geranium in front is labelled to show which two strains were its parents.

The anthers have been removed from a white petunia flower and are being used to pollinate a purple flower.

When the stigma is ready, pollen from the male strain is brushed on. After the flowers are pollinated, the breeder must wait for weeks to find out if his choice of parent strains for the new hybrid was good. First the seeds must ripen. Then they have to be planted, and the plants have to grow to maturity to see what they are like. A breeder may try many crosses of different parent strains before finding a combination that works.

Fields of Flowers

Once a good hybrid has been developed, the two parent strains must be grown in large numbers. The work of actually developing new hybrids takes place mostly at nurseries in the United States, Holland, Germany, Denmark, and England. It can take pounds and pounds of seeds of the parent strains to produce the thousands of plants needed to raise hybrid seed for sale. Because of the need for good growing conditions and for so much hand labor, the hybrid seed crop is usually grown in countries where the climate is moderate and workers don't expect high pay. The seeds of the parent strains are planted in greenhouses in the mountain regions of countries like Kenya in Africa, Thailand in Asia, and Guatemala in Central America. Then their flowers are cross-pollinated by hand, and the seeds are sent back to the seed companies in the United States.

Not all the flowers grown for seed are hybrids. Some are open-pollinated. That means the flowers are all grown out-of-doors and are allowed to be pollinated naturally. Most of these varieties are grown in fields in California. It takes much

Overleaf: Fields of colorful flowers lie in front of greenhouses at Goldsmith Seeds in Gilroy, California.

less work to raise them than it does the seeds for hybrid
varieties.

Growing Flowers for Cutting

While seed companies are growing vast fields of flowers
for seed to sell, flower farmers are producing flowers that will
be sold to florist shops. Customers, in turn, will buy those
flowers to beautify their homes.

Roses, chrysanthemums, and carnations are the three
most popular cut flowers in the United States. All of them
need controlled heat to bloom reliably, so they must be pro-
tected while growing, in a greenhouse or covered area. Marigolds, daisies, dahlias, and sweet William, however, can be
grown outdoors in fields.

Carnations growing in a ventilated greenhouse in California.

THREE
Many Kinds of Flowers

The variety of flowers is enormous, with colors, scents, and shapes to please everyone. Strangely enough, not all flowers are what they seem.

Simple Flowers and Composite Flowers

A flower such as a rose is called a simple flower, even though it looks very big and has many petals. It is called "simple" because what we see is just one flower, with the male and female parts surrounded by petals.

A daisy, however, is another story. It may look simpler to us than a rose, but it is really much more complicated. The yellow center of the daisy isn't only one flower. It is really hundreds of very tiny flowers. The flowers that fill the center have very small petals. The ones around the edges have large petals. Flowers like this—dandelions are another example— are called composites, since each flower is actually composed of many small ones.

Like roses, dianthus has simple flowers. Each blossom is one complete flower.

Composite flowers are much more efficient from the plant's point of view than simple ones. One visit from an insect can pollinate hundreds of flowers rather than just one, so the plant can produce large numbers of seeds more easily.

Flowers from Faraway

Most flowers that we grow in our gardens are simple, like roses, or composite, like daisies. But there are other sorts

Poinsettias come from the American tropics, but today they grow wild as big bushes in Hawaii.

of flowers, too, especially in the tropics. While they look like flowers to us, they are really more complicated. Other parts of the plant besides the petals, pistils, and stamens help make up what we call the flower. For example, the "petals" of the poinsettia, which we see at Christmastime, are not petals at

Daisies are composite flowers. When a bee visits the blossom, it can pollinate many flowers at once.

all. They are actually special leaves around the flowers, called bracts, that turn red when the flowers bloom.

The anthurium blossom is also more than a flower. The "tongue" in the center is actually a spike of many tiny flowers. The large "petal" surrounding the spike is really a bract.

A Tropical Place for Tropical Plants

Tropical flowers are becoming more and more popular in North America. Most areas of the continent are too cool and dry to grow these beauties outdoors, so they must be raised in heated greenhouses that are kept moist. In Hawaii, however, the temperatures are warm enough and the air is humid enough that tropical plants can be grown outside. Since greenhouses are expensive to build and heat, raising tropical plants in Hawaii is much cheaper than in other parts of the country.

Anthuriums were brought to Hawaii in 1859 from Central America, where they grow wild. The climate and the volcanic soil of the big island of Hawaii turned out to be perfect for these exotic blossoms. Today, anthuriums come in many different colors. Most of the varieties were developed by Hawaiian growers. Growing anthuriums in Hawaii is a million dollar business, and the long-lasting blooms are sent all over the world from there.

Many beautiful flowers are native to Hawaii, too, and the people use necklaces of flowers, called leis, as a greeting for guests and new arrivals on the islands. It takes dozens of

The anthurium "flower" is really a flower spike set off by a large, colored bract.

flowers to make a typical lei. Flowers with lovely scents, such as gardenias, plumaria, and some orchids, are favorites for leis.

Leis are made by stringing flowers or parts of flowers together.

Fragrant plumaria blossoms are favorites for making leis.

FOUR
The Amazing Orchids

The orchid family is the largest family of flowering plants. Orchid variety is immense, with sizes ranging from very tiny to almost a foot across. Orchids come in every imaginable color except black.

Kinds of Orchids

Orchids come in a variety of fanciful forms, too. There are orchids that look like Santa Claus, Dracula, a monkey, and a spaceman. At least one is shaped like a butterfly, including "antennae." This orchid flower, atop a long, thin stem, bounces in the breeze like a flitting butterfly.

One reason for the variety of orchid forms is the differences among their pollinators in nature. A few are pollinated by hummingbirds, bats, or the wind, but many use flies or unusual types of bees to carry pollen from one flower to the next. The shape of the flower often serves to attract the insect by fooling it. The centers of some look like female bees, for

Different kinds of orchids.

example, which attract male bees. Others form elaborate traps which make the pollinator struggle to get free, thereby picking up the pollen on its body as it tries to escape.

Orchids from Seeds

Orchids have the smallest seeds in the world. They look like fine powder. It would take more than 1,500 orchid seeds to fill a teaspoon. Unlike other seeds, the tiny orchid seed doesn't have stored food to feed the young plant before it grows green leaves. In nature, orchids depend on funguses to help them grow. The people who raise orchids spread the seeds inside a bottle on a special gelled growing medium that contains sugar. The sugar feeds the little plants.

It takes a long time for orchid plants to get started. After the seeds are placed on the growing medium, the bottle is closed for six to seven months. At the end of that time, a tiny forest of three to four hundred baby orchid plants crowd the bottle.

The young plants are then thinned so that there are only about twenty in each bottle. When the plants are about a year and a half old, they are only an inch or so tall.

Plants from Plants

It takes a lot of work and many years to get flowering plants from orchid seeds. This makes developing hybrid seeds impractical. And because the traits of the female parent and the male parent of the seeds will have combined in the new plants, no one can be sure what the flowers will look like

An orchid seedpod. The fine powder consists of hundreds of orchid seeds.

After the small plants are thinned, they grow in a new bottle until they are about eighteen months old.

These five orchids grew from seeds in the same pod. You can see that they are quite different from one another.

until they bloom. For these reasons, it is just too expensive and chancy to grow large numbers of orchid plants for sale from seeds.

Luckily, there is another way to reproduce orchids, a way of making new plants just like the old ones. This method is a form of cloning, a word for making new plants or animals identical to a single parent. In cloning, cells are taken from one plant and made to grow into a complete new one.

Cloning can be done in several different ways. Here's how it's done with orchids. First, a growing shoot is cut from the plant. The leaves are stripped away, revealing the tiny bit of tissue, called the meristem, that would grow the next year. The cells making up the meristem are special. Under the right conditions, they can grow into every part of an adult plant. To clone orchid plants, the meristem is cut out. Then it is put in liquid in a flask. The flask is placed on a machine that rotates it in the light. Plants normally respond to gravity by sending roots downward and shoots upward. But when the meristem tissue is rotated, it can't sense "up" and "down," so it ends up growing into a lumpy green clump of cells. It takes about two months for the meristem to grow into nice big clump of cells.

The clumps of cells can be cut up and placed in new

Flasks containing bits of orchid tissue are rotated on this machine.

When the clumps are placed on a growing medium, they send out roots and shoots and grow into orchid plants.

flasks, where they grow into new clumps, and so forth. At this stage, it takes only two or three weeks for the new clumps to form. This process can be repeated over and over for as long as eight years until there are thousands of clumps from just one plant. When a clump is removed from the rotating flask and placed on a growing medium, it will act like a normal plant and produce roots and shoots. After the roots and shoots have formed, the plants are sorted and planted. Eventually, they will produce beautiful orchid flowers.

FIVE
Not Only from Seeds

Orchids aren't the only plants that can be grown without seeds. Some plants, like tulips, clone themselves naturally by growing new bulbs underground along the edges of the old one. Others can be multiplied easily by the grower by cutting off a stem or leaf from the plant and getting it to form roots, making a new plant.

Crazy about Tulips

In about 1554, tulip bulbs first reached Europe from the East. Soon, hyacinths joined them. Within a hundred and fifty years, all the great estates of Europe featured beautiful bulb gardens, with the beds arranged in fancy designs.

The Dutch went crazy over bulbs, paying unbelievable prices, often for just one bulb. In 1624, a single bulb of a white tulip with red stripes brought an amount equal to $1,600 today. It was a good investment, for a year later the price had more than doubled! By 1636, one of them cost the equiv-

alent of $13,000. This sort of mad speculation couldn't go on forever, and the next year, the bottom fell out of the bulb market. Many people lost their fortunes, but the collapse brought sanity to the flower business.

While western Europe was going crazy over bulbs, they were also highly valued in Constantinople, capital of the Ottoman Empire. Tulips could only be bought and sold inside the capital city. Every spring there was a glorious tulip festival during the full moon. The guests had to wear clothes that matched the flowers, and countless tulips stood in vases filled with colored water. It was an unforgettable sight.

Secrets Underground

Many favorite flowers come from bulbs or from tubers, swollen underground roots or stems that store food for the winter. Tulips and daffodils both grow from bulbs. The plants die down in the fall. Under the ground, the fat bulbs contain stored food to nourish the plants when they sprout again in the springtime. Just like a seed, the bulb has a miniature plant inside.

Tubers are different from bulbs. They don't have a formed plant inside. Instead, they have spots where the new growth will begin in the springtime. Dahlias are popular flowers that store their energy during the winter in tubers.

Each year, bulbs reproduce themselves underground. Plants like dahlias produce more tubers. The grower or gar-

Bicolor tulips like these once sold for fabulous sums.

The round bulbs on the left are from tulips. To the right is a daffodil bulb. Notice the smaller bulbs growing from its base. At the bottom is a clump of dahlia tubers with the old stem attached.

Dahlias are popular flowers that grow from tubers.

dener can dig up the bulbs or tubers and separate them to get new plants.

Making Plants from Plants

The easiest way to grow more geraniums and some other plants is by cuttings. The grower cuts shoots from a plant and puts them into a potting mixture. The shoots must be kept moist until they grow roots so they don't dry out, since

Martha Washington geraniums.

roots are the main way plants gather moisture. Once the shoots have rooted, they can be potted individually.

Making new plants from cuttings is a form of cloning. The new plants will be just like the parent plant from which the cutting was taken.

SIX
The Harvest

Whether plants are grown for their seeds, as bedding plants to be sold to grow in home gardens, as house plants, or for cut flowers, the final product must find its way to the customer.

Gathering in the Seeds

Once the seedpods have ripened, the seeds must be collected. For some flowers, like marigolds, this is simple. A machine with vacuum hoses is run down the rows. The hoses suck in the dry seeds that are ready to be released. They also suck in soil. After being harvested, the seeds must be cleaned of dirt.

Seeds of some flowers must be picked by hand. The seedpods of impatiens must be harvested as soon as the seeds are ripe. If they are left on the plants too long, they will burst, scattering the seeds on the ground.

Many seeds sold in packets are grown by the companies

that developed the varieties. These commercial seed companies then sell the seeds in large quantities to other companies that package the seeds and sell them to home gardeners. The commercial companies also sell seeds to the nurseries that grow plants to sell to home gardeners.

Plants for Sale

Every spring, many stores set up garden shops to sell plants. The seeds are planted into plastic packs with four or six compartments, called ponies. The plants are carefully watered and cared for until they are big enough to sell. Most of the plants sold in pony packs are grown in huge greenhouses in Michigan, a central location with a flower-growing tradition.

Greenhouse growers across the country grow houseplants for florists to sell. Flowering houseplants need to be shipped just when they begin to flower so that the buyers can enjoy as many flowers as possible.

Floral Beauty

Growing cut flowers to sell can be tricky. The flowers must be cut at just the right stage, usually just as they are opening. Then they must be marketed as quickly as possible so they stay fresh.

Big cities like San Francisco have flower markets three times a week. The market starts before dawn, so the growers

Verbena seeds being harvested.

Thousands of plants in pony packs being grown for sale in stores as bedding plants.

must get up very early to get their flowers to the market. Florists come to the flower market and choose the flowers they will take to their shops to sell.

Many different kinds of flowers are available at the flower

market. Plants can be bought there, too. Some of the flowers were grown in fields nearby, while others come from greenhouses. Most of the exotic flowers have been shipped by air all the way from Hawaii.

Modern transportation allows us to buy beautiful flowers from Hawaii and bedding plants from the Midwest. We can purchase seeds for the newest varieties of colorful blossoms produced by careful breeding at commercial seed companies. With all the flowers available today, everyone can enjoy having flowers at home, both inside the house and in flowerboxes or out in the garden.

These cyclamen plants will be sold to florist shops.

Cut carnations ready for market.

Flowers for sale at the San Francisco flower market.

Flowers in Your Home

If you pick flowers from your garden or buy some at the store, you will want them to last as long as possible. When you bring the flowers inside, run some water into the sink. Then hold the stems of the flowers underwater while you cut off the ends. Cutting them underwater makes it easier for the stems to carry water to the blossoms. It keeps air from clogging the tiny water pipelines inside the stems.

Some flowers, such as roses and daffodils, do best if put into warm water. You can buy a special powder at the florist shop that will help your flowers last longer when dissolved in the water. Be sure you check the water level every day or two, since the flowers are drinking it up.

By bringing flowers into your home, you can add some of nature's beauty to your daily life, even if it is snowy or cold outside.

GLOSSARY

anthers—knobs on the tops of the stamens that carry the pollen

bracts—leaves around the flower that can be brightly colored, making them look like petals

cloning—reproducing organisms in ways, such as taking cuttings from plants, that produce new individuals just like the old ones

composite flower—a blossom such as a daisy that is made up of many tiny flowers

cross-pollination—transfer of pollen from one flower to a different flower

cuttings—pieces of plant shoots rooted in potting mix to make new plants

embryo—the tiny new plant inside the seed

hybrid seed—seed produced by crossing two different strains of a species. The resulting plants are all very similar.

lei—a necklace made of flowers, used to greet guests in Hawaii

meristem—the growing tip of a new plant shoot. Meristem cells can grow into any part of the plant.

open-pollinated flowers—flowers left alone to be pollinated naturally

ovaries—inner female part of the flower where the egg cells are

perennial—a plant that lives for several or more years

pistil—the female part of the flower that can be seen; the stigma is at the end of the pistil

pollen—fine grains from the male part of the flower that fertilize the eggs after pollination

pollination—transfer of pollen from the male to the female parts of flowers

simple flower—a blossom such as a rose that consists of just one flower

stamens—the male parts of the flower that carry the anthers

stigma—the sticky surface on top of the pistil where pollen grains stick during pollination

tubers—swollen underground roots or stems that store food during winter and sprout new shoots in the spring

INDEX